Charles Chalmers

Electro-Chemistry with Postive Results

SALZWASSER
VERLAG

Charles Chalmers

Electro-Chemistry with Postive Results

Reprint of the original, first published in 1859.

1st Edition 2022 | ISBN: 978-3-37513-246-0

Verlag (Publisher): Salzwasser Verlag GmbH, Zeilweg 44, 60439 Frankfurt, Deutschland
Vertretungsberechtigt (Authorized to represent): E. Roepke, Zeilweg 44, 60439 Frankfurt, Deutschland
Druck (Print): Books on Demand GmbH, In de Tarpen 42, 22848 Norderstedt, Deutschland

ELECTRO-CHEMISTRY,

WITH

POSITIVE RESULTS.

(In which it is demonstrated that there is a Latent Electricity existing in bodies, as well as a Latent Heat; and that those bodies, when deprived of their Latent Electricity, indicate a change in their characteristic properties.)

BY

CHARLES CHALMERS,

LATE OF MERCHISTON ACADEMY.

—

A REPRINT.

—

LONDON:

JOHN CHURCHILL, NEW BURLINGTON STREET;

MACLACHLAN AND STEWART, EDINBURGH;

AND G. AND R. KING, ABERDEEN.

1859.

ADVERTISEMENT.

THE experiments by which I have demonstrated that a latent electricity exists in bodies, cannot be explained by Chemists in accordance with their previous teaching ; and the tubes that I require for the successful performance of those experiments are fusible with difficulty while under the action of a powerful blowpipe, but which resist fusion when subjected to the strongest heat of a common fire. The tubes to which I refer were exhibited in the Crystal Palace of Hyde-Park. They were afterwards disposed of to Opticians in London, and to others in the country. They were thicker in the glass, and less fusible than the tubes which are usually sold as Bohemian glass. I with difficulty procured a few of those tubes, and it was with those that I successfully performed my experiments. A transverse section of the tubes with which I operated is here represented.

C. C.

MERCHISTON CASTLE BANK,
Edinburgh, Nov. 1859.

ELECTRO-CHEMISTRY,

WITH

POSITIVE RESULTS;

AND

NOTES ON THE TWO ELECTRICITIES.[*]

---

1. ARE the two electricities material elements?

The late Dr. Turner, in his Elements of Chemistry, states that the "effects of electricity are so similar to those of a mechanical agent—it appears so distinctly to emanate from substances which contain it in excess, and rends asunder all obstacles in its course so exactly like a body in rapid motion, that the impression of its existence as a distinct material substance, *sui generis*, forces itself irresistibly on the mind. All nations, accordingly, have spontaneously concurred in regarding electricity as a material principle; and scientific men give a preference to the same view."

2. If electricity is regarded by scientific men as a material principle, how comes it that they have

---

[*] The substance of this tract is embodied in a pamphlet which I published at the close of 1849, entitled, "Thoughts on Electricity."

made it an exception to the other material elements, by assuming, without proof, that it does not combine with those elements, as those elements combine with each other? It cannot be because of its imponderability, as heat, an imponderable element, is known to enter into chemical combination with the ponderable elements of nature.

3. Is it so, that the two electricities are material elements, and that they are not an exception to the common law; that they combine with the other material elements as those elements combine with each other; and that compound bodies are decomposed by the two electricities precisely as the ponderable elements decompose those bodies—namely, by respectively combining with the constituents of the body which is under decomposition; and thus in all electro decompositions, those bodies which are given off at the positive wire, are given off in combination with the positive electricity of that wire, and those given off at the negative wire are given off in combination with the negative electricity of that wire? And, therefore, when a compound body is decomposed by electricity, we do not obtain the constituents of that body, but new compounds—the two electricities having respectively combined with the constituents of the body which has been decomposed. Accordingly, in the decomposition of a neutral salt

by electricity, we do not obtain the constituents of
that body, but new compounds. One of the constituents of the salt having combined with positive
electricity, a compound is formed, possessing properties different from either of the constituents, an acid
being the product : the other constituent of the salt
having combined with negative electricity, a compound is formed, possessing properties different from
either of the constituents—an alkali being the product ; and in order to obtain the constituents of the
decomposed salt, we would require to disunite positive electricity from the acid, and negative electricity
from the alkali.

EXPERIMENT 1.

4. My first experiment in corroboration of these
views was made ten years ago, an account of which
was published at the close of 1849. Aware that
heat impairs the affinity which subsists between the
constituents of a compound body : " that in the high-
est conceivable degrees of heat, chemical combination
does not take place;" and that, in some instances,
compound bodies, such as ammonia, the peroxide of
manganese, the oxide of chlorine, and the oxides of
mercury, silver and gold, are decomposed by heat,—I
therefore inferred, that were two bodies, the one
united with positive and the other with negative
electricity, subjected to an intense heat, the two elec-

tricities, viewed as material elements, would have
their affinities for the bodies with which they were in
combination so loosened or impaired, that they would
unite when connected with each other by means of a
platinum wire, or any other conductor of electricity.
With this view I employed a cast iron tray, twelve
inches in length, ten in width, and three in depth. I

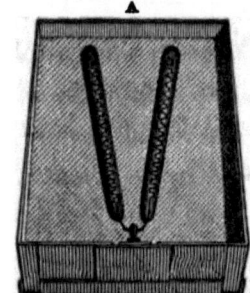

FIG. 1.

covered the bottom of the tray with a mixture of
plaster of Paris and finely-sifted coal-ash, and upon the
surface of this mixture I placed two thick glass tubes,
hermetically sealed, the one containing a portion of
the chlorate of potassa, and another an equivalent
quantity of potassium. These tubes were connected
internally with each other by means of platina wires,
one of which was introduced into the chlorate of
potassa in the one tube, and the other into the potassium in the other. The position of the tubes in the
tray are represented *Fig.* 1. I now filled the tray
with plaster of Paris and coal-ash, and upon this

mixture I placed an iron plate, on which were laid two weights, forty pounds each. The tray with the weights was placed on a common fire, the fireplace of which was so constructed, that an intense heat might at any time be produced. As oxygen would come off from the chlorate of potassa, when the temperature of that salt was raised, I inferred that the intense heat to which the oxygen and potassium would be subjected, would disunite positive electricity from the oxygen, and negative electricity from the potassium; and that the two electricities thus set free would escape by the platina wires, and unite with each other, heat being the product. After the tray which had been brought to a red heat had cooled down sufficiently, I proceeded to examine its contents. Both tubes were entire. I opened at one extremity the tube which contained the potassium, a portion of which fell out, and presented very much the external characters of carbon. Its metallic lustre was gone; and when thrown upon water, there was neither combustion nor action of any kind. I introduced a sharp-pointed wire into the tube, with a view of extracting what remained of the potassium; but the instant that I touched the potassium with the wire, the whole exploded in my hand. How is it that the properties and external characters of this substance were so very different from the properties

and external characters of potassium? Is it that
potassium, deprived of its negative electricity, pos-
sesses properties and external characters, such as I
have described? I now examined the contents of
the other tube. It was evident that oxygen had
been disengaged from the chlorate of potassa, and
that the residual constituents were those of the
chloride of potassium. The only other change which
had taken place was, that the surface of the tube
appeared to be bedewed with moisture.

5. This first experiment was an earnest of what I
might realise when provided with a suitable furnace
and blow-pipe apparatus, and with those tubes which
resist an intense heat, without fusion and without fracture. In the prosecution of my experiments, I found
that flint glass tubes were not suitable, as they contained lead in their composition, which renders them
easily fusible, and the materials which I introduced
into them were generally blown out, or a rupture of
the tubes took place. From some difficulty, which I
could not explain, I failed to obtain, though every
effort was made on my part, those tubes which resist
fusibility while exposed to an intense heat. Having,
however, partially succeeded in my first experiment, I
persisted in operating with such tubes as I could procure, unsuitable though they were, resolved either to
verify my views on electro-chemistry, or prove them

fallacious ; and it was not until after years of toil and failure, I at last obtained a positive result, which proves that there is a latent electricity existing in bodies as well as a latent heat.

EXPERIMENT 2.

6. At the close of 1856, I procured *one* of those German glass tubes that are fusible with difficulty, a transverse section of which is represented in *Fig.* 2., indicating its thickness of glass and calibre, and into which, when sealed at one extremity, I poured a small portion of nitric acid ; but as another tube was required, I substituted a tube of iron, into which I introduced a few grains of caustic potash. Both tubes were hermetically sealed, and contained platina wires, which were not joined together externally as is represented in *Fig.* 1., but were kept apart from each other, and made to project beyond the tray, through two small perforations in one of its sides, as is represented in *Fig.* 3.

FIG. 2.

FIG. 3.

The iron tube deposited in the tray was insulated by inclosing it in a tube of glass, while the platina wires which passed through the small perforations in the side of the tray were encased in capillary tubes. The extremities of the wires which projected beyond the tray dipped into a small bent tube that contained a solution of the iodide of potassium. In every other respect the experiment was conducted precisely as that which I had performed in 1849. In the course of the experiment, I found that when the tray was brought to a red heat, the solution of the iodide of potassium was decomposed; the iodine was first made manifest in the limb of the bent tube into which the wire from the tube in the tray containing the *nitric acid* was introduced. From what source was the electricity derived by which the iodide of potassium was decomposed? There can be no escape, I should think, from the conclusion that the positive electricity was derived from the acid, and the negative electricity from the alkali. I obtained precisely the same result by introducing into a similar bent tube, containing iodide of potassium, the platina wires from a water battery. The iodide was decomposed, and the iodine first made itself visible in the limb of the tube into which the positive wire from the battery was introduced.

7. The materials with which I operate are neces-

sarily so very small in quantity, particularly when I introduce liquids into glass tubes, that the results, though positive, may be thought trivial. Thus when I introduce nitric acid into a glass tube, I first fill it with acid, which is afterwards decanted, and the tube is kept inverted until all the acid has dropped from it, leaving only as much acid as adheres to the platinum wire and the internal surface of the tube. The quantity of acid which remains is not more than two grains, or one grain and a half; if more than this, the rupture of the tube, when exposed to an intense heat, generally takes place. It indeed requires a nice adjustment in respect to the quantity of the materials with which I operate, as well as the requisite hardness and thickness of the tubes which I employ, in order to resist, without fusion and without fracture, the degree of heat to which, in the course of my experiments, they are subjected.

8. In October 1857, I obtained what I had hitherto failed to procure—a few of those German glass tubes of the thickness and hardness that I required ; and I now proceed to detail those experiments in which the iodide of potassium, contained in the small bent tube, was decomposed by electricity, of which the positive electricity was derived either from an acid, or from oxygen or iodine, and the negative electricity

from a metal or an alkali; thus proving that positive electricity is in combination with the first class of bodies, or what are called the supporters of combustion, and negative electricity with the second class, or what are called combustible bodies.

Experiments with Tubes of German Glass, fusible with great difficulty.

EXPERIMENT 3.—October 22, 1857.

9. Iodide of potassium, decomposed by electricity; the positive electricity derived from nitric acid, and the negative electricity from sodium.

Two tubes, hermetically sealed, were put into the tray, (*Fig.* 3.) both of which were embedded in a mixture of plaster of Paris and finely-sifted coal-ash. One of the tubes contained about two grains of nitric acid, and the other an equivalent quantity of sodium. From the interior of these tubes, platina wires projected beyond the tray, and to prevent the wires from coming in contact with the iron of the tray, they were encased in capillary tubes. These wires were introduced into a small bent tube, external of the tray, containing a solution of the iodide of potassium (*Fig.* 3.) After the tray had been brought to a red heat, the solution itself being kept at a low temperature, the iodide was decomposed; the iodine appearing in the limb of the bent tube, into which was introduced the extremity of the wire which projected from the tube in the tray that contained the acid. It is evident that electricity was the agent by which the iodide was decomposed, and as the iodide first appeared in the limb of the tube into which the wire from the acid was introduced, the positive electricity was derived from the acid, and consequently the negative electricity from the metal.

EXPERIMENT 4.—December 18, 1857.

10. The iodide of potassium, decomposed by electricity, of which the positive electricity was derived from nitric acid, and the negative electricity from potassium.

Two grains of nitric acid were introduced into one of the tubes, and an equivalent quantity of potassium into another. In every respect the experiment was conducted as before, and with precisely the same result.

EXPERIMENT 5.—January 2, 1858.

11. The iodide of potassium decomposed by electricity, of which the positive electricity was derived from oxygen, and the negative electricity from potassium.

Two grains of the chlorate of potassa were introduced into one of the tubes, from which oxygen by means of heat was evolved, and an equivalent quantity of potassium into the other. In the decomposition of the solution in the bent tube, the iodine was first made apparent in the limb of the tube into which was introduced the extremity of the wire which projected from the tube in the tray that contained the oxygen, which indicates that the positive electricity was derived from the oxygen, and consequently the negative electricity from the metal.

EXPERIMENT 6.—January 16, 1858.

12. A solution of the iodide of potassium was decomposed by electricity, of which the positive electricity was derived from iodine, and the negative electricity from potassium.

Six grains of iodine were introduced into one of the tubes deposited in the tray, and two grains of potassium in the other. When the tray was brought to a red heat, the solution of the iodide in the bent tube was decomposed, and the iodine of the solution was first made apparent in the limb of the bent tube into which the wire was introduced that projected from the iodine contained in the tube deposited in the tray.

13. In all these experiments in which the iodide of potassium was decomposed, the iodine of the solution first became apparent in the limb of the tube into which the wire from the tray was introduced in connection with the tube that contained nitric acid, or oxygen, or iodine; which proves that those bodies, when subjected to an intense heat, have their positive electricity, with which they are united, disengaged; and that sodium and potassium, and the alkali caustic potash, have, in like manner, the negative electricity disengaged, with which they are united.

14. I have thus demonstrated by these experiments, *all of which* (with tubes that stand an intense heat without fusion and without fracture) *I pledge myself to perform*, that iodine, oxygen, potassium and sodium, are not simple but compound bodies; that in those bodies there are imponderable elements in combination with ponderable elements, and that when deprived of their imponderable elements, they indicate a change in their characteristic properties.

I had now exhausted my supply of those tubes of

German glass which, for hardness and thickness, are available for those experiments, and I must now wait for another supply before I can resume my inquiry into the *positive changes* which take place in bodies when deprived of their respective electricities.

15. It is obvious that the decomposition of the iodide of potassium does not indicate that the bodies which have decomposed it are wholly deprived of the electricity in combination with them. With a view to withdraw positive electricity absolutely from the acid, and negative electricity from the potassium, I coupled the tube containing the acid which had been used in the decomposition of the iodide, with a tube containing a fresh supply of potassium, and connected their platina wires with each other, as is represented in *Fig.* 1, and inferred that the negative electricity, in combination with the potassium, would withdraw, when the tray was brought to a red heat, what remained, if any, of the positive electricity of the acid ; and in like manner I coupled the tube containing the potassium, which had also been used in the decomposition of the iodide, with a tube containing a fresh supply of acid, and inferred that what remained of the negative electricity, in combination with the potassium, if any would be withdrawn by the positive electricity of the acid.

16. The views that I have advanced at the commencement of this Tract on Electro-Chemistry, and the experimental results which I have obtained in corroboration of those views, render the following experiments by Sir H. Davey on the "Transfer of Elements," intelligible.

17. When three cups, N, I, P, *Fig.* 4, are arranged as represented in the woodcut, and the negative wire from a powerful battery is introduced into cup N,

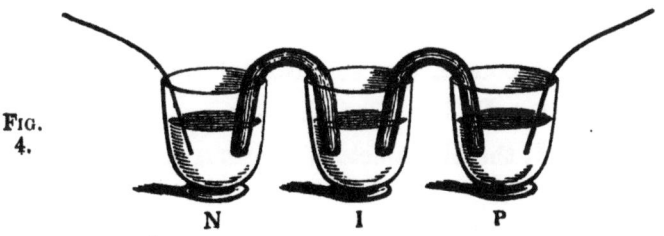

Fig. 4.

and the positive wire into P, the three cups being connected by means of amianthus—how is it, that when a solution of a neutral salt is put into I, and distilled water into the cups N and P, the neutral salt is decomposed, and in every instance the acid base of the salt is decanted into P, and the alkaline base into N?*

The ponderable constituent of the acid in the solution of the neutral salt is attracted to the positive

---

* According to the view taken in these notes, of the composition of acids and alkalies, the term *base of the acid* or *base of the alkali* is applied to the ponderable elements of those bodies.

wire in the cup P, and there combining with positive electricity, resumes the properties of the acid; and the ponderable constituent of the alkali is attracted to the negative wire in the cup N, and there combining with negative electricity, resumes its alkaline properties.

18. When N is filled with a solution of the sulphate of potash, and the cups I and P with distilled water, the water in I being tinged with a solution of litmus, how is it that, in the decomposition of the sulphate of potash, the acid base of the salt is transferred to cup P, but in passing through the intermediate cup I, the blue tincture of litmus does not assume a red colour?

The constituents of a neutral salt possess neither the properties of an acid nor those of an alkali; when, therefore, the sulphate of potash in the cup N is decomposed, the acid base of the salt has not yet acquired the properties of an acid—it has not yet combined with positive electricity; it therefore passes through the solution of litmus in the intermediate cup I, without changing its blue colour into red; and is decanted into cup P, where it combines with positive electricity, and has its acid properties restored. If the contents of the cup P be now poured into the intermediate cup I, the blue tincture of the litmus will assume a red colour.

19. When the cup P is filled with a solution of the sulphate of potash, and the cups N and I with distilled water, the water in I being tinged with turmeric, how is it that in the decomposition of the sulphate of potash, the alkaline base of the salt, in passing through the intermediate cup I on its route to N, does not change the colour of the turmeric?

In the decomposition of the salt, the alkaline base does not possess alkaline properties; it has not yet combined with negative electricity; it therefore does not change the colour of the turmeric in its passage through I. When, however, it reaches the cup N, it there combines with negative electricity, and has its alkaline properties restored. If the contents of the cup N be now decanted into I, the colour of the turmeric will undergo the characteristic change.

20. When the cup I is filled with a weak solution of ammonia, the cup N with a solution of the sulphate of potash, and distilled water is put in the cup P, the sulphate of potash is decomposed; the acid base of the salt being set free, is attracted by the positive wire to the cup P, but in its passage through I it produces no chemical change upon the solution of ammonia; a combination does not take place between the ammonia and the acid base which passes through it. How is this?

The sulphate of potash in the cup N is decomposed, and the acid base of the salt set free is attracted towards the cup P; but in passing through the intermediate cup, it does not combine with the ammonia and form a neutral salt, because the alkali in I requires to give off its negative electricity before its ponderable constituent can combine with the ponderable constituent of the acid. The ponderable constituent of the alkali has a greater affinity for its imponderable element than it has for the acid base that passes through it. There is therefore no chemical change upon the solution of ammonia in the cup I. When, however, the acid base of the sulphate of potash reaches the cup P, it there combines with positive electricity, and has its acid properties restored. If the solution in P, which is now a solution of sulphuric acid, be decanted into I, the positive electricity of the acid will unite with the negative electricity of the alkali, heat being the product; and the residual constituents of acid and alkali will now combine and form a neutral salt, namely, the sulphate of ammonia.

21. When a solution of the nitrate of potash is placed in the cup P, distilled water in N, and sulphuric acid in I, the nitrate of potash is decomposed, and the alkaline constituent of the salt is drawn through the cup I without undergoing any change

itself, or causing any change in the acid. What is
the reason of this?

The alkaline constituent of the salt when it enters
the cup I, containing sulphuric acid, does not combine with that acid. The sulphuric acid requires to
be disunited from its positive electricity before it can
combine with the alkaline base of the salt. When,
however, the alkaline base passes to cup N, it there
unites with negative electricity, and has its alkaline
properties restored. If now the alkaline solution in
N be poured into cup I, the positive electricity of
the sulphuric acid will unite with the negative electricity of the alkali, and the base of the acid and
the base of the alkali will now unite and form a
neutral salt.

22. When a solution of the sulphate of potash is
put into the cup N, distilled water in P, and a solution of baryta in I, the sulphate of potash is decomposed, and the base of the acid, one of the constituents of the salt, is attracted by the wire in P, and
is liberated; but the base of the acid does not pass
through the solution of baryta as it passed through
the solution of ammonia, but combines with the base
of baryta, and is precipitated. How is this?

The base of baryta has the greatest affinity for
the base of sulphuric acid, insomuch that it separates
the base of that acid from all the alkalies and alka-

line earths with which it combines, namely, from
strontia, potassa, soda, lime, magnesia, and ammonia.
To account, therefore, for the precipitate in I, the
base of baryta having a greater affinity for the base
of sulphuric acid than it has for the negative electricity with which it is united, the baryta is decomposed, the negative electricity is set free, and the
base of the acid is arrested in the intermediate cup
I, by combining with the base of baryta, and because
of this a precipitate of the sulphate of baryta takes
place.

23. When an acid and an alkali are brought into
contact, how is it that great heat is evolved and a
compound formed, possessing neither the properties
of an acid nor an alkali?

The acid, in combining with an alkali, gives off
its positive electricity, and is thus deprived of that
which imparted to it the properties of an acid; and
the alkali, in combining with an acid, gives off its
negative electricity, and is thus deprived of that
which imparted to it alkaline properties; and because of this a compound is formed by the combination of the ponderable constituents of the acid and
alkali—possessing neither alkaline properties nor
those of an acid, and the great heat evolved is consequent upon the union of the two electricities which
are given off.

24. If a platinum capsule, which contains a solution of caustic potash, be connected with one wire of an electrometer, and a slip of platinum connected with the other wire is dipped into nitric acid, and introduced into the potash, why does the capsule in contact with the alkali indicate the presence of negative, and the slip of platinum in contact with the acid indicate the presence of positive electricity?

The acid, in combining with the alkali, gives off its positive, and the alkali, in combining with the acid, gives off its negative, electricity; and therefore the slip of platinum in contact with the acid indicates the presence of the former, and the platinum capsule in contact with the alkali the presence of the latter, electricity.

25. In double decompositions, as in the case of the two neutral salts when they decompose one another, in which the acid base of the one combines with the alkaline base of the other respectively, how is it that these combinations give rise to no heat, and no current of electricity?

When an acid and an alkali enter into combination and form a neutral salt, they give off their respective electricities, heat being the product; and therefore in double decompositions, when the two neutral salts decompose one another, and enter into new combinations, the constituents of these salts have no electricity to give off, and because of this they give rise to no heat and no current of electricity.

26. When an acid decomposes a neutral salt by combining with the alkaline base of the salt, how is it that the acid base which is set free has its acid properties restored? The acid which decomposes the neutral salt, in combining with the alkaline base of the salt, gives off its positive electricity to the base of the acid which is liberated, and because of this the acid base which has been set free has its acid properties restored. In the same manner the alkali which decomposes a neutral salt gives off to the alkaline base which is liberated its negative electricity, and because of this the alkaline base which has been set free has its alkaline properties restored.

APPENDIX.

NOTES ON THE TWO ELECTRICITIES.

APPENDIX.

NOTES ON THE TWO ELECTRICITIES.

———

The electricity which is made manifest by the electrical machine, is not derived from the ground, as some have supposed, but from the machine itself. In Sturgeon's lectures on electricity, the following statements are made.—"When the cushion is in metallic connection with the ground, by means of the copper wire, or when the hand is placed on it, it gets an abundant supply from that source." Again: "I have already stated in a former lecture, that the insulated cushion or rubber of a machine, yields but a small portion to the revolving glass, because of a want of supply from the ground." Also, in one of our standard works on Chemistry, it is there stated, that "when one conductor is uninsulated, the electricity derived from the other is proportionably augmented, in the positive conductor, because then the other draws uninterrupted supplies from the earth."

The following experiment proves that this opinion is erroneous. I thoroughly insulated the electrical machine which I made use of in my experiments. I interposed a sheet of gutta-percha, one of the best insulators of electricity that is yet known, between the machine and the table on which it stands. Moreover, the machine itself had no electrical communication with the ground, by means of a chain or otherwise. Into the upper part of each conductor I inserted a brass wire, the other extremity of which terminated in a brass ball. The wires with the balls were made to bend towards each other. (Fig. 5.)

Fig. 5.

With this addition to the machine, the glass cylinder was made to revolve, and immediately a constant succession of sparks took place between the balls at the extremities of the bent wires; and I find that this succession of sparks can be maintained for any length of time without intermission; and, as the machine was thoroughly insulated, the electricity must have been derived, not from the ground, but from the machine itself. But some have supposed, after having seen the above experiment, that the electricity must therefore be derived from the atmosphere. This opinion is also erroneous.

From the negative and positive balls of the conductors I made to project metallic points or needles, (Fig. 6,) and

FIG. 6.

inferred that if the machine derived its electricity from the atmosphere, that the balls with the metallic points

would withdraw more electricity from that source than
before, and, therefore, a larger supply of electricity
would now be made visible between the balls at the
extremities of the bent wires. Upon turning the handle
of the glass cylinder, the sparks between the balls at the
extremities of the wires, and which previously could be
maintained for any length of time, without intermission,
now entirely ceased. The electricity had thus been
withdrawn from the machine, and given off to the
atmosphere, by means of the conductors with the metallic
points. I, therefore, infer that it is neither from the
ground, nor from the atmosphere, that the electricity is
derived, but from the machine itself.*

From what source, therefore, does the machine derive
its electricity? When the union of the two electricities
takes place, *heat* is the product. I, therefore *synthetically*
infer that heat is a binary compound, of which the
elements are the two electricities; and as the electricity
of the electrical machine is neither derived from the
ground nor from the atmosphere, but from the machine
itself, I, therefore, *analytically* infer that the heat which
is excited by the friction of the rubber upon the glass
cylinder is decomposed; the heat being interposed between two bodies, of which one has an affinity for

---

* When the balls at the extremities of the bent wires are made
to approach each other, sparks between the balls will then take
place; the attraction of the two electricities, consequent upon the
proximity of the balls, being now much greater than the attraction
of the electricity at the metallic points for the induced electricity
of the atmosphere, which takes place at those points.

positive and the other for negative electricity; the glass of the cylinder being the one which attracts and carries off the positive electricity, the silk of the rubber the other which attracts and gives off the negative electricity.

Wherefore I also infer that when a body is charged with one of the two electricities, and electrical induction takes place in the body to which it is presented, the heat at the surface of the induced body is decomposed, of which one of the constituents is attracted and the other repelled by the proximity of the body that is charged with one of the two electricities.

I may state one or two examples of electrical induction, as I conceicve they ocur in nature. When a cloud charged with one of the two electricities passes over the spire of a church, the spire, by electrical induction, is charged with the opposite electricity; and when the attraction of the two electricities, that of the cloud and that of the spire is such, as shall overcome the low conducting power of the atmosphere, the electricity of the cloud descends and unites with the electricity of the spire; and thus in common parlance, the spire is said to be struck with lightning.

Again: When a cloud charged with one of the two electricities passes over the surface of the ocean, it induces the opposite electricity in the water beneath, and because of the attraction of the two electricities, that of the cloud and that of the water beneath, the water rises above its level towards the cloud, and the

cloud in a column descends; and thus is exhibited one
of the modifications of that remarkable phenomenon of
what is called a water-spout.   (Fig. 7.)

FIG. 7.